If Rapunzel Were Rachelle

By Angela Davis

Illustrations by Izzy Bean

Printed in the United States of America

ISBN 978-1-948270-09-0

Keen Vision Publishing
www.keen-vision.com

This book is dedicated to my dad, Jerry Davis. Thanks for your loyalty to your family. Your hard work inspires us all. Thanks for continuously encouraging me to take a leap, Daddy-O.

Love, Baby-O

Once upon a time, there was a man and a woman who had longed for a baby since the day they were married. When the woman was with child, they were so overjoyed. Their dream of becoming parents would finally come true. They couldn't wait to see their beautiful, brown, bundle of joy.

One day, the woman became ill and bedridden. The man called his grandmother for help. His grandmother told him to make his wife a smoothie using purple cabbage, blueberries, and an African eggplant. In desperation, the man quickly went to the store to get all the items. He found everything except the African eggplant.

While taking a run in the neighborhood, the man found a garden filled with African eggplants. He was so elated that he ran over and took some eggplants from the garden without wondering who they belonged to. He couldn't believe his prayers had been answered. After gathering as many as he could carry, he ran home and made the smoothie for his wife. Within a few days, she was completely healed. Everything went back to normal, and the couple continued to prepare for the arrival of their baby.

One day, there was a knock on their door. When they opened the door, they saw a little old woman. The old woman had long, straight, gray hair and looked very angry. "You!" the woman shouted at the man as she shook her cane at him. "You took my eggplants out of my garden! Why do you think you can come into my yard and take what is mine?"

"It was for my wife," the man explained. "She was very ill and we needed the eggplants. We couldn't find one anywhere."

"She doesn't look sick to me." The old woman scowled.

"Because of your eggplant, I am healed. Now, I can have our baby." The woman explained. "I'm so sorry. I promise to make it up to you. Is there anything I can do to repay you for the eggplant? We will do whatever you ask."

The little old lady thought for a moment and said, "Did you say you were having a baby? "

"Yes," responded the couple.

The little old woman smiled. "Okay. Well on the day the baby is born, you will give her to me."

"No!" the couple shouted. "We cannot do that!"

"You promised me anything," the old woman said with a grin. The couple looked at each other and sobbed.

On the day the baby was born, the man and woman decided to keep it a secret so that the old woman wouldn't take their baby. Unfortunately, the little old woman had been watching them from her window.

All the villagers came to visit the couple and their baby. As everyone was admiring the baby, there was a loud, long rap at the door. The couple looked at each other with fear. They knew it was the old woman coming to take the baby. One of the neighbors opened the door, and the old woman wobbled in on her cane. The entire room was so quiet that all anyone could hear was the pounding of the old woman's cane on the floor.

The old woman walked up to the couple and snatched the baby from their arms. The couple cried uncontrollably. The little old woman cradled the baby in her arms and began to walk out the door.

Before she closed the door, she turned to the couple and asked, "What did you name her?"
"Rachelle," the couple squeezed out through their tears.
"Rachelle?" the old woman said. "Hmmm, I guess that will do."

Rachelle brought the little old woman so much joy. She loved Rachelle so much. She did not want her happiness to ever go away. She didn't let Rachelle go out to play because she was afraid that the young couple would one day come back to steal Rachelle away. So she built a tower some miles away from the village. The tower had no doors and only one window. No one could find them, and if they did, there was no way they could come in.

Rachelle grew to be a beautiful child. She was bubbly and quite the charmer. She always knew exactly what to say to make the old woman's day. Rachelle had one distinct feature that no other child had. She had big, beautiful, outstanding hair. Her hair was round with perfect curls. Her hair grew so wide that the little old woman had to widen the tower.

The more Rachelle grew, the bigger her hair became. The old woman knew that if she made the tower any wider, someone would notice it. So, she decided to straighten Rachelle's hair so that it could hang from the window. It took the old woman weeks to straighten all of Rachelle's hair. Once it was done, Rachelle's hair was so long that it draped from the very top of the tower all the way down to the ground.

As Rachelle got older, there was no longer enough room for the little old woman, Rachelle, and Rachelle's hair. So, the little old woman moved back to the village and left Rachelle alone in the tower. The little old woman used Rachelle's hair to get out and into the tower.

One day, Rachelle felt a tug on her hair. She got excited because she assumed it was the little old woman. Being alone in the tower was no fun, so Rachelle was always excited to see the little old woman. To her surprise, her visitor was not the little old woman at all. It was a prince!

"Who are you?" Rachelle asked.

"I am a prince. I live far away from your village," the prince explained. "I have been traveling along that path over there. When I saw your long mane draping from the window, I had to see who it belonged to. I've never seen anything like it. Your hair is so beautiful and amazing."

Rachelle smiled with joy. Her entire life, she had never seen anyone other than the little old woman. Making a new friend made Rachelle very happy. The prince and Rachelle became great friends. He came to see Rachelle every day, and the two of them laughed and told each other jokes.

One day, the little old woman saw the prince heading up to see Rachelle. She began to panic.

"What if he tells some of the villagers about Rachelle," the little old woman thought to herself. "Soon enough, the word will get to her parents and everyone will know where I've been hiding her. Then, they will come to take Rachelle away!"

The little old woman dashed up the hill to run the prince away. "Rachelle, Rachelle, let down your long mane!" The little old woman shouted.

Rachelle let down her hair and smiled at the little old woman. "Oh, I am so glad to see you." Rachelle smiled. She reached out to give the little old woman a hug, but the old woman pulled away from her.

"Rachelle, you must never allow the prince into this tower again. Do you understand?" The little old woman snapped.

"I never have anyone to talk to!" Rachelle cried. "You always leave me here in the tower alone, and I get so lone—"

"Never!" The old woman cut her off. "I said never! Do you understand, Rachelle?"

"Yes ma'am," Rachelle sobbed.
Rachelle got into bed and cried herself to sleep.

The next day, Rachelle heard a familiar voice saying her name. It was the prince making his daily visit. Rachelle looked around to make sure the old woman wasn't watching, then let down her hair so that the prince could climb up.

"Rachelle, you look sad." The prince said. "What's wrong? I would do anything to make you happy again."

Rachelle told the prince about the little old woman's request. This deeply saddened the prince. He knew he had to help Rachelle find an answer to her problem. The two of them walked in circles around the tower in deep thought. Finally, the prince asked, "Why is this tower so wide?"

Rachelle explained that her hair was so big, before it was straightened, that the little old woman had to widen the tower so all her hair would fit.

"That's it!" The prince cried.
"Your hair! She can't get back in without your hair!"

Rachelle smiled.
She knew what she had to do.

The next morning, the little old woman arrived at the tower and did not see Rachelle's long mane. "Rachelle, Rachelle," she called. "Let down your hair."

Rachelle appeared with spiraled coils of curls. The little old woman was furious. "What have you done to your hair?"

"I washed my hair," Rachelle replied. "Now it's not straightened. You'll have to come back at another time." Rachelle walked away from the window with a smile. The little old woman was even more upset, but she did not want to startle Rachelle and make her do something drastic. So, the little old woman walked away.

The next day, the little old woman came back to the tower with a plan. She had a fishing rod with her. She swung the hook up into the window and hooked Rachelle's coiled hair. Then, she reeled Rachelle's coil to her. Rachelle's hair stretched all the way to the bottom of the tower. The little old woman climbed up Rachelle's hair.

"Thanks for letting me in Rachelle," the old woman said snidely.

The old woman let Rachelle have it. She told her that she was wrong for what she had done and that no one should ever come up the tower again. Rachelle did not understand and questioned the old lady about why she had to stay up there forever. Rachelle pleaded to be allowed to go down the tower and asked so many questions that the little old woman became confused and frustrated. Finally, the little old woman yelled, "Because your mother and father will find you and take you back!"

Rachelle was so shocked and filled with sadness that she fell to the floor and began to cry. The little old woman tried to explain. She told Rachelle what her mother and father had done. Rachelle was very quiet. She refused to speak to the old woman.

The little old woman tried to comfort Rachelle by combing her hair. She put Rachelle's hair in Bantu Knots to make sure Rachelle would not let anyone up the tower. Before the little old woman left, she warned Rachelle to never let the prince up the tower again or she would be punished. The little old woman hated talking to Rachelle this way, but she was so afraid of losing her.

The next day, the Prince arrived. Rachelle explained the news of her parents to him. He promised to find her parents in the village. Rachelle assured him that if he found her parents, he could have her as his wife. Determined to marry Rachelle, he saddled off into the day. The prince was confident that he would find Rachelle's parents.

The little old woman arrived at the tower later that day with a pogo stick. "Rachelle, Rachelle, unravel your Bantus."

Rachelle did as she was told. The little old woman attached Rachelle's hair to her pogo stick and bounced through the window.

Rachelle was filled with so many emotions. On one hand, she was excited that her parents might come to rescue her. On the other hand, she was very upset with the little old woman. She could not believe that the little old woman she had always known and loved had such a dark past. Rachelle became very impatient waiting on her parents and the prince. She knew she had to do something to get out of the tower.

"You know," Rachelle said to the old woman. "I forgive you for what you did. You have always been good to me. Why would you keep this secret from me?"

The little old woman became very silent. She didn't know what to say to Rachelle, so she said nothing at all. This made Rachelle angry. She began to shout and cry.

"Fine!" Rachelle yelled. "You don't have to say anything! It doesn't matter now! I will never find my parents! After all these years, I know that they have had other children! They've forgotten all about me and it's all your fault!"

The little old woman did not like to see Rachelle cry. "Rachelle. I'm so sorry. I never meant to hurt you." The old woman apologized. "What can I do to make you feel better? I will do anything."
"Anything?" Rachelle asked.

"Yes," the little old woman cried.
"Anything you want, Rachelle. Just please stop crying."
"Okay, well straighten my hair back out," Rachelle requested.
"No!" shouted the little old woman.
"But you said anything," Rachelle said calmly.
The words sounded so familiar to the little old woman. She
knew she had been tricked. She quietly began straightening
Rachelle's hair. When she was done, she quietly left. No words
were spoken.

After the old woman left, Rachelle felt liberated. She gave herself the Big Chop. Once she finished cutting all her hair off, she tied it to the top of the tower and let it drape down to the ground. Suddenly, she heard the prince calling her name.

"Oh, Prince." She cried. "I'm afraid for you to see me. I look a little different now, but I had to do what I had to do."

"Rachelle, I don't care. I love you anyway you are. Please let me see you!"

To his surprise, Rachelle slid down the long mane of hair right into his arms. He laughed. "Did you do something different with your hair?" he chuckled.

They both laughed and hugged. They were so happy that they could be together.

"Let's go!" Rachelle shouted.

"What about your hair?" The prince asked.

"Let's just say it's a parting gift for the little old woman." Rachelle said with a smile.

The two of them saddled the prince's horse and rode off into the sunset.

The next day, the prince had a surprise for Rachelle. He had arranged a wedding and everyone was there to see it – even her parents! The prince had found them in the village. They never forgot about Rachelle. In fact, they were so sad that they couldn't bring themselves to have another child. When the prince told them that he had found Rachelle, they were overjoyed. When they saw their beautiful daughter, they just hugged her and cried. After the wedding, Rachelle, the prince, and Rachelle's parents lived happily ever after.

THE END

ABOUT THE AUTHOR

Hello! My name is Angela Davis. Having taught elementary for the last 10 years, I have always had a love for children's books. Recently, my daughter got the opportunity to live out her dreams by acting in a Broadway play. I was so inspired by how young she is and already living out her dreams, that I decided to live out mine. It has always been my dream to be an author. Writing has been an outlet for me. I write because books can help children build self-esteem, escape, connect, love, inspire, and dream. This is what books did and still do for me. I love helping children, and books are a great way to do this. Whether about bullying, friendships, or daily troubles, sometimes the best lessons are taught through a book.

If Rapunzel Were Rachelle is my first book. This book is a spin on the fairy tale, *Rapunzel*. It is my goal to develop a book series about princesses that relate to people of color, who are more modern and connect to today's kids. This book was written to inspire confidence, love, beauty, and dreams. I would like to eventually have a doll and book package set sold in stores.

I am thankful for my family who encourage me to do my best. My daughter inspires me and I must do the same for her. This book is my "leap of faith." I am a firm believer of God's word, "For I know the plans I have for you, plans to prosper you and not to harm you, plans to give you hope and a future," Jeremiah 29:11.

STAY CONNECTED

Thank you for purchasing *If Rapunzel Were Rachelle*. Angela would like to connect with you! Below are a few ways you can connect with Angela.

FACEBOOK Angela Denise Davis

INSTAGRAM @angeladavisauthor

WEBSITE angela-davisauthor.com

EMAIL anndvs25@aol.com